To Ben and Vitti, with love   HC

For Tara, Alexandra and Adam   KH

PUFFIN BOOKS

Published by the Penguin Group
Penguin Books Ltd, 80 Strand, London WC2R 0RL, England
Penguin Putnam Inc., 375 Hudson Street, New York, New York 10014, USA
Penguin Books Australia Ltd, 250 Camberwell Road, Camberwell, Victoria 3124, Australia
Penguin Books Canada Ltd, 10 Alcorn Avenue, Toronto, Ontario, Canada M4V 3B2
Penguin Books India (P) Ltd, 11 Community Centre, Panchsheel Park, New Delhi – 110 017, India
Penguin Books (NZ) Ltd, Cnr Rosedale and Airborne Roads, Albany, Auckland, New Zealand
Penguin Books (South Africa) (Pty) Ltd, 24 Sturdee Avenue, Rosebank 2196, South Africa

Penguin Books Ltd, Registered Offices: 80 Strand, London WC2R 0RL, England

www.penguin.com

First published by Aurum Press Ltd 1985
Published by Viking 2001
3 5 7 9 10 8 6 4 2
Published in Puffin Books 2001
3 5 7 9 10 8 6 4

Copyright © HIT Entertainment plc, 2001
Text copyright © Katharine Holabird, 1985
Illustrations copyright © Helen Craig Ltd, 1985

Angelina, Angelina Ballerina and the Dancing Angelina logo are trademarks of HIT Entertainment plc,
Katharine Holabird and Helen Craig Ltd. Angelina is registered in the UK, Japan and US Pat. & Tm. Off.
The Dancing Angelina logo is registered in the UK.

Manufactured in China by South China Printing Ltd. Co.

British Library Cataloguing in Publication Data
A CIP catalogue record for this book is available from the British Library

ISBN 0–670–91154–2 Hardback
ISBN 0–140–56863–8 Paperback

To find out more about Angelina, visit her web site at **www.angelinaballerina.com**

Angelina at the Fair

Story by Katharine Holabird Illustrations by Helen Craig

PUFFIN

All winter Angelina had been saving her pocket money for the wonderful day when the fair would come again. When she wasn't busy dancing, she would sit by her window and daydream about the big wheel and the roller coaster. She liked all the most exciting rides.

At last, when all the snow had melted and the wind
was soft and warm again, the May Day Fair arrived in
town. Angelina's ballet class performed a maypole
dance at school in celebration of spring, and Angelina
almost flew around the maypole she was so excited.
All the parents watched and cheered.

After the dance Angelina was ready to go to the fair with her friends, but her parents stopped her. "You've forgotten that little cousin Henry is visiting today," said Angelina's father. "He will be very disappointed if he can't go to the fair with you."

Angelina was furious. "I don't want to take Henry!" she said. "I hate little boys!" But Henry held out his hand just the same, and Angelina had to take him with her. The music from the fair was already floating across the fields and Angelina's friends had gone ahead. She grabbed Henry's hand and dragged him along behind her, running as fast as she could.

At the entrance to the fair was a stand of brightly coloured balloons. "Oh, look!" cried Henry. "Balloons!"

But Angelina didn't pay any attention. "We're going on the big wheel," she said. The big wheel was huge and Henry was frightened, but Angelina loved the feeling of flying up in the air, and so they took two rides.

When they got off Henry felt sick, but he cheered up when he saw the merry-go-round. "Look!" he said. "Can we go on that?"

"Not now," said Angelina. "We're going on the fast rides." She took poor Henry on the roller coaster. Henry shut his eyes and held on tightly as the little car zoomed up and down the tracks. Angelina loved it and wanted to go again, but Henry wasn't sure he wanted to take any more rides at all.

Then Angelina saw the Haunted House.
"I'm sure you'll like this," she said, and pulled
Henry inside.

A big spider dangled just above
their heads as they went in …

and a skeleton jumped out
and pointed right at them.

When they bumped into a ghost
Angelina reached out to touch Henry ...

but he was gone!

"Henry, Henry!" Angelina called, but there was no answer in the darkness. Angelina hurried back through the Haunted House trying to find him.

She looked everywhere until she got tangled up in
the spider and had to be rescued by the ticket seller.

Angelina couldn't see Henry outside the
Haunted House either. She ran through the
crowds looking for him. She ran past all the rides
and all the games, but Henry was nowhere to
be found. At last she was so worried and upset
that she sat down by the entrance to the fair and
began to cry.

And there, watching the balloon man blow up the beautiful balloons, was Henry! Angelina was so relieved that she gave him a big hug and a kiss. "What is your favourite colour, Henry?" she asked. Henry chose a blue balloon.

"What would you like to do now?" Angelina asked kindly.

Henry said he would like to go on the merry-go-round,

so they went on three times and they both loved it.

Afterwards they had a double chocolate ice cream and walked home slowly together. "I like fairs," said Henry, and Angelina smiled.

"You can come with me any time," she said.